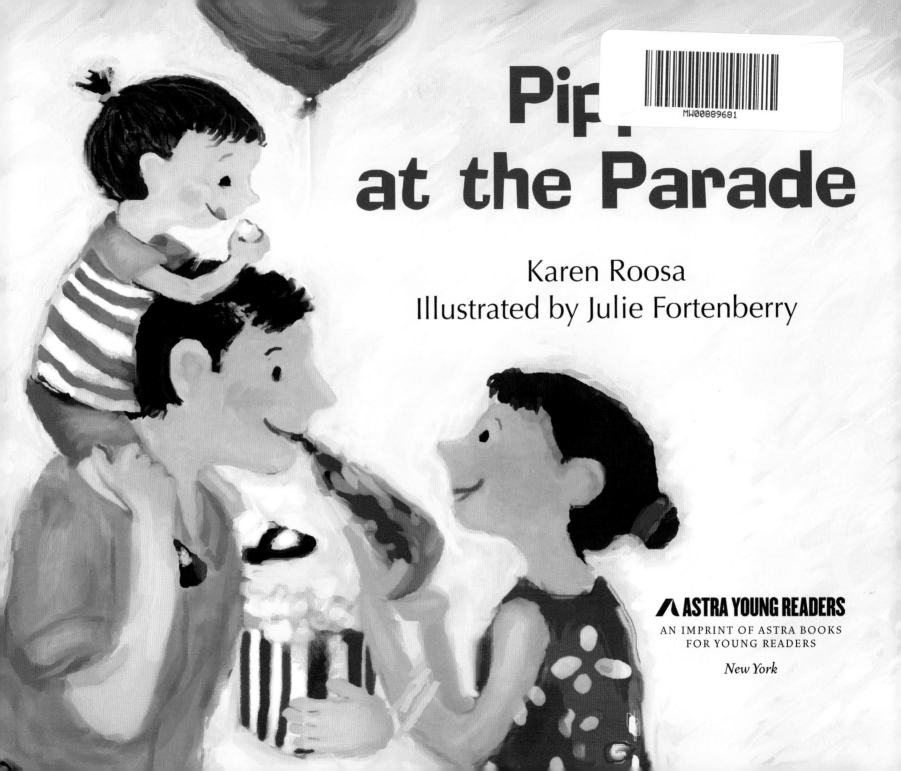

Pippa at the Parade

Karen Roosa
Illustrated by Julie Fortenberry

ASTRA YOUNG READERS

AN IMPRINT OF ASTRA BOOKS
FOR YOUNG READERS

New York

Pippa's toes tap,
feel the beat.
Music starting
down the street.

Clapping hands!
Clappity-clap.
Band is coming!
Tippity-tap.

See them marching,
strutting along,
stepping lively
to the jazzy song.

Shiny trumpets,
brasses blare!
Trombones swaying,
debonair.

Drummers drumming,
rat-a-tat-tat,
ta-tiki-ta-ta,
rat-a-tat-tat.

One, two,
three, and four,
around the corner—
here comes more!

Handspring! Cartwheel!
Dive and dip.
Soaring gymnast
does a flip!

Mighty giant,
ten feet tall!
Man on stilts,
after all.

Pizza, popcorn
in the tummy.
Candy apples,
very yummy.

Bright balloon
in the big, blue sky,
sailing higher.
Wave good-bye.

Toss a ball,
win a prize.
Pippa throws.
Big surprise!

Cotton candy,
sticky sweet,
on Pippa's fingers—
tasty treat.

Yellow! Orange!
Fireworks flare.
Boom, ka-boom
in the evening air.

Light is fading.
Sunset red.

Parade is over.
Time for bed.

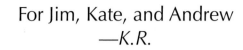

For Jim, Kate, and Andrew
—*K.R.*

For Don, John, and Annie
—*J.F.*

For information about permission to reproduce selections from this book,
please contact permissions@astrapublishinghouse.com.

Astra Young Readers
An imprint of Astra Books for Young Readers,
a division of Astra Publishing House
astrapublishinghouse.com
Printed in Atlanta, Georgia

Library of Congress Cataloging-in-Publication Data

Roosa, Karen.
Pippa at the parade / Karen Roosa ; illustrated by Julie Fortenberry. — 1st ed.
p. cm.
Summary: A young child has a fun-filled day with her parents at the big parade.
ISBN 978-1-59078-567-6 (hardcover : alk. paper)
[1. Stories in rhyme. 2. Parades—Fiction.] I. Fortenberry, Julie, ill. II. Title.

PZ8.3.R6656Pi 2009
[E]—dc22
2008028127

First edition

Designed by Tim Gillner
The illustrations are done digitally.

10 9 8 7 6 5 4 3 2 1